# Bob 'n John

## IN
## BAD TO THE BONE

## BY MARILYN SADLER • ILLUSTRATED BY ROGER BOLLEN

WHISTLESTOP ®

Troll

Bob and John lived in a lovely neighborhood at
the end of South Paw Boulevard.

Every morning they had their milk in the flower
garden behind their house.

John loved the sweet smell of honeysuckle and
the beautiful song of the robins. Bob loved the milk.

John worked very hard in the garden. He prepared just the right mix of soil. He carefully arranged each plant by size and color. Then he showed Bob where to dig the holes.

It was usually lunchtime before they finished with their work. Bob put his shovel away as soon as he heard the can opener.

After lunch, Bob and John retired to the front porch, where John enjoyed his easy-listening music, and Bob napped on the porch swing.

The afternoons were reserved for a walk through the neighborhood. They never traveled very far, however, because John liked to talk to the neighbors.

Next to gardening, John's great love was cooking.
Dinner was usually one of John's fancy French
dishes. Although Bob didn't know what he was
eating, it never seemed to stop him.

Bob and John went to bed as soon as it was dark. They wanted to get up early, so that they could have their milk in the flower garden behind their house.

Bob and John had the perfect life. Then, one day, something happened to change all of that.

Two little dogs moved into the house next door.

The dogs were from Canine Park. They moved to South Paw because they wanted a house with a backyard.

John was not very happy. "The neighborhood's going to the dogs," he complained.

The next morning, Bob and John were having their milk in the garden, when their peace and quiet were suddenly interrupted by the sound of digging. One moment later, a clump of dirt landed in John's glass.

Bob lifted John up to look over the wall. The dogs were digging holes all over their backyard. "Maybe they're planting a garden," said Bob. But John knew better.

"Make no bones about it," he said. "They're not planting a garden."

After lunch, Bob and John moved to the front porch. John hoped that his music would relax him. The dogs did not like John's music, however, and they began to bark.

Bob and John left for their walk early that
afternoon. John had a lot to tell the neighbors.
But when the dogs saw them, they chased Bob
and John all the way down South Paw Boulevard.

When Bob and John got home that night, it was dark. John did not feel like fussing over dinner, so he fixed some tuna a la Paw Paw. They were just about to eat, when a breeze blew through the window. Expecting the sweet smell of honeysuckle, John was horrified when he smelled dog food.

After that, John could not eat his tuna a la Paw Paw, so Bob ate it for him.

That night, John dreamed that dogs had taken over the neighborhood. When he woke up, he was happy to know that it was just a bad dream. Then he heard the digging.

The digging continued throughout the week. Finally, John got his earmuffs out of storage. Although he couldn't hear the digging, he couldn't hear his easy-listening music, either.

John did his best to control himself, but he was getting hot under the collar.

Then, one afternoon, John was whipping up a chocolate mouse in the kitchen. Suddenly, he saw his pansies and buttercups go flying by the window.

He looked outside and, to his horror, found the
dogs digging holes in his flower garden.

RRRRRRRRR

John flew out of the house in a rage. He was screaming like a wildcat, and his mixer was still running. For the first time that week, the dogs stopped digging.

The dogs were so frightened by the look of John,
they tore out of the yard. Yipping in a frenzy, they
raced toward the safety of their own backyard.

The next day, the dogs moved back to Canine Park.
Bob and John could not believe their great fortune.

That morning, Bob and John celebrated by putting their garden back in order. Every time Bob dug his shovel into the earth, he hit a bone.

Nothing was going to upset John, however. He was in far too good a mood. After all, he had a fresh glass of milk. The smell of honeysuckle was everywhere. And the dogs were gone.

"There's nothing worse," John told Bob . . .

". . . than two little yapping dogs!"